By
Minyetta Bailey

THE COST TO LOVE

FORGIVENESS

MOCY PUBLISHING
WWW.MOCYPUBLISHING.COM

Detroit, Michigan

Printed by CreateSpace, An Amazon.com Company

THE COST TO LOVE: FORGIVENESS

ISBN 978-1-940831-38-1
Copyright © 2017 by Minyetta Bailey

Published by Mocy Publishing, LLC.
Website: www.mocypublishing.com
Email: info@mocypublishing.com

The Cost To Love Pt. 2 Forgiveness

by

Minyetta Bailey

Dedication

This book is dedicated to the greatest love of my life. You came into my world exactly when I needed you. You have given me way more than what was taken from me. At the same time to helped restore me & pushed me to my greatest limit of the exploration of what love truly is. When I say to you that I love you, I hope you truly know that I am sincere in ever letter used in the expression. And not only do I want you to hear these words and receive them, I also want to show you that I mean them in every way, shape, form or fashion by the way of my actions.

I love you truly. This is dedicated to my one and only's.

C.A.B.W
& D.B.

Introduction

In the world we live in A lot of people use the word love in the right context but in the wrong shape, form and fashion. This is written as a gesture to show you what the word love really means.

The Cost to Love Pt.2

FORGIVENESS

Will Star forgive her fiancé for not telling her the truth from the beginning? How could he have done this to her? What was she supposed to do? Where would they go from here?

Chapter One

Star sat dumb founded, sitting on the edge of the bed staring at the business card with Darren's information on it. She didn't know what to make of this situation, but as always she had started to over think what was going on. Darren knew about what had happened to her. Did Darren have something to do with what had happened to Star when she was younger? Did Darren know and just not say anything? Or maybe Darren had no clue? Could this all have been part of some sort of plan? What was Darren's role in all of this? Or did he even have a part?

Star started to think about her and Darren's relationship. Was this all a ploy? Did Darren really love Star or was this just a game he was playing? What was going on and what was going to happen? The more Star sat there and thought to herself, the more frustrated she became. What was this that she was living? Was it even real? What was all of this for?

Darren exited the bathroom area with a towel over his head, when he looked up he saw Star sitting on the edge of the bed looking at something in her hand.

To Darren, Star looked mighty focused. "What was Star looking at that had all of her attention?" Darren thought to himself as he crept up behind Star and glanced over her shoulder. When Darren saw what Star was looking at in her hands he immediately held his breathe as if that would make him invisible in the room but he couldn't help but make a noise when he swallowed hard.

When Star heard the noise over her shoulder, she turned to look to see what the noise was and saw Darren standing there looking shook. Like he had seen a ghost or something. By the expression on Darren's face Star could tell that he knew something and didn't want Star to find out. Star could tell that Darren was guilty of something she just didn't know what so she started with questions. Star got up off the bed, stood to her feet while looking at Darren and began to sob.

Star was crying because now she had the chance to look at the man that she thought and knew she was in love with in the face after she believed that he was lying to her. Star had the chance to see Darren in a whole new light. Star cried because she was hurt. That is what it boils down to. Hurt from and by the things that she had already started to believe in her head while piecing the information together.

Star had to know or atleast she wanted to know so in the midst of her tears she started questioning Darren. Star was so emotional and frustrated at the same time that she wasn't talking to Darren, she was yelling. The stupid question is always the first to come out before the woman lets the man know how smart she is or how smart she thought she was.

"What the fuck is this?" Star asked Darren holding the piece of paper that contained Darren's business information even though Star already knew what the piece of paper was. She still asked anyway to see if Darren was going to be honest with her as well as to see what his answer was going to be.

Darren looked at Star puzzled. He didn't understand what was going on neither why it was happening, he just knew he had a lot of explaining to do to Star but he could barely get a word in to answer what Star was asking him.

Between all the yelling that she was doing. Each time Darren went to answer one of Star's questions, she either continued yelling at him and or asked Darren another question.

Darren wanted to give Star all the information that he knew, he just wanted Star to calm down so he could atleast explain himself to see if Star would see where he was coming from in all this fiasco but he couldn't. The longer it took Darren to speak or say a word the quicker it seemed to piss Star off. Star had become angrier in her delivery and with her words. Star had even begun to yell louder if that is even possible.

Darren was embarrassed. He had wanted to tell Star what he had known for some time now. He just didn't know how to bring it to her. Darren was so caught up in making Star smile and happy that he just couldn't bring himself to open his mouth to speak the words. Darren knew once he told Star what he had known and that he had known this information for some time now that he had the chance of losing Star.

The possibility of losing Star, the woman that he had fell so madly and deeply in love with scared him. So Darren kept the information to himself. It had been years now to where Darren didn't even think two things or two times about the situation anymore. Darren had become accustom to keeping that information hidden from Star until he felt it was the right time to tell her. If ever he did decide to tell Star.

Before Darren proposed marriage to Star, he thought that marrying Star would be the beginning of their next chapter in life. With Star carrying his last name. Darren thought that the two of them would be able to start writing their happily ever after story to someday be able to tell. Darren had long thought about as well as planned this out.

He wanted to keep Star so busy enjoying life that she had no time to think about the bad stuff that had happened to her when she was younger. Whether it was the situation with her mother's murder or the situation that had happened to Star as a teenager. Darren didn't want to remind Star of things that made her sad or made her cry.

When Darren finally proposed marriage to Star and she accepted, he was the happiest man on earth. But during the wedding planning process, Star had sunk into a depression about not having her mother as well as not knowing what truly happened to her and why she was murdered. This would have been a good time to tell Star what he had known but seeing the state of mind that Star was already in, Darren didn't want Star to completely fall of the edge of the cliff, so Darren chose not to tell her.

But vowed to help Star find out or recover as much information as possible. That is how the first private investigator got involved. Darren hired him to find out the information that Star wanted. In the process of seeking the private investigator, Darren could see a total three hundred and sixty degree change in Star. From her attitude to her appearance. Depression is an ugly thing to deal with and face when it is happening to your mate and you feel helpless.

Star had started to smile again and be lively. Meaning that she was happy again and knowing that Star was happy again made Darren happy as well.   That is all Darren wanted for Star was to keep her happy and enjoying life.   Darren had done many things for Star in the pursuit of helping her stay happy.   Darren knew that in order to keep Star that way he had to help her find the true happiness that she seeked.

That would be his only agreement with the whole situation because Darren knew that if Star found out the real information or the true details and facts that it wouldn't make her happy.   That it could possibly destroy Star or even Darren himself for that fact.   Darren definitely thought it was going to destroy their situation together and the possibility of the two of them getting married.

Chapter Two

Darren didn't want to chance that, so when Darren and Star found a suitable private investigator, suitable only to Darren because he and the private investigator had previously meet and discussed what Darren wanted the private investigator to do and how Darren wanted it done. Darren told the private investigator that he wanted the investigator to meet with him first to discuss what he had found. Then once Darren knew all that the private investigator had found out.

Darren would decide what was suitable or what information he wanted Star to know. Very sneaky and devious for Darren to go behind Star's back to try to keep her from finding out the truth but Darren was willing to go as far as it took even if it took money. That is how Darren kept the first private investigator from telling Star the whole truth. Darren was paying him off which means that Darren was paying the first private investigator in multiple ways.

First Darren was paying the private investigator to uncover information just to see if what the private investigator was uncovering was true because Darren already knew all of the facts and details himself.   Then he was paying the private investigator again for not telling Star the whole truth.   I don't know about you but that seem like a wealthy ass lie.

Darren was willing to pay people money to make sure nobody including Star didn't find out the truth.   Darren must have had money to just throw away because that is exactly what he was doing by having to keep paying off the private investigator, when Darren could have simply told Star the truth and or what he knew.

Star had no clue of what Darren was doing behind her back. She also had no reason to question Darren or doubt him.   Ever since they had been together, Darren went out of his way to put and keep a smile on Star's face and Star knew that.   Darren had done everything right from the beginning of their relationship.

In the process of sweeping her off her feet and if it was a game, Darren had won.   That is the reason Star was here right now with Darren. That was the reason Star had agreed to the proposal of marriage when Darren asked and said yes. That was another reason why Star loved this man. But what had Darren been doing? Even at the point of standing in the bedroom with the piece of paper, Star still had no clue.

Star was asking a hell of a lot of questions. To where Darren couldn't keep up. In the process of Star being angry, Darren still didn't want to upset her even more then she was so he kept his mouth shut. Darren had to realize what Star was asking him to do. Which was be honest and keep it real with her. But was Star ready for what she was asking for? Was Star ready to know the truth or was she just putting on a show?

If Darren decided to tell Star the truth, would she be able to handle it? Would Star be able to bear it and overcome? Or would she let it break her back down to where she would be depressed about life herself again? Darren had questions too. But his questions were not merely as important as what Star was asking. Darren didn't know what to do?

All he knew was not to speak until he was ready and until he felt that Star was ready to hear what Darren had to say.

All the while, Star was yelling, Darren was listening and paying attention to her but proceeded to walk over toward his closet to grab something to wear. Once he was dressed, Darren tried to console Star but she wasn't having it. She was furious and over the top with anger and frustration.

Star could not calm down and with every single second Star grew angrier.Star was so frustrated that her eyes began to well up with tears. The more Star shouted, the faster Darren moved in dressing himself because he didn't know where this situation was headed but he wanted to make sure that he was fully dressed just in case he had to make an escape while Star was being belligerent.

Darren didn't want to leave but he could see that the situation was not getting any better. Star had blown her gasket and the hood of her car was smoking. Darren could see it as well as he could tell that she was not calming down any time sooner. Darren didn't know where to start in the argument and or which question to answer first.

All Darren knew was that nomatter what was going on, he was willing to stay and help Star with the healing that she needed as well as with the healing of their relationship if Star was willing. At the moment Darren didn't see a glisten of light at what they would call or consider the end of the tunnel. Star was at the edge of the cliff and she wasn't willing to fall but had already jumped off the cliff head first without any safety gear, landing gear or parachute.

Star didn't seem to be calming down and she could even feel her body temperature rising. Star's heart beat was beating at a quick pace, faster than usual. She could feel the inside of her palms beginning to sweat to the point that she had to leave her hands open just to let the air grace past them. Star's leg was shaking as if she was nervous or had some type of disorder with staying still.

Along with the shaking of the leg, Star also begin to grit her teeth in the efforts to keep herself from saying anything that she didn't mean or would regret in the future in the midst of being angry. But that didn't happen. As soon as Star felt the tear welling up in her eyes, the pain & frustration from what was going on in the inside of Star and she tried to form the words to express herself but it just seemed that Star was having a mental breakdown.

A nuclear meltdown that Darren knew that he had something to do with and helped cause. Darren still didn't know what to do or how to calm Star down. It seemed that the more Darren tried to calm the situation, the more that it wasn't working or helping Star. It was more like adding gasoline to the already burning out of control inferno. Darren tried everything he thought that he should and once he was done and out of options, there was only one conclusion that he knew he didn't want to do but really didn't have any other choice in the matter but to do it, which was leave.

Darren would leave only to give Star the space that he wasn't sure that she needed. But he knew that this would be the only way to get to her. As well as a way to get her to calm down so that they could atleast discuss what had happened and what was now going on.   Darren crept closer and closer toward the door in efforts to leave as Star's head begin to twist around as if in the scene from the movie The Exorcist.

Darren didn't want to leave but he had no other choice.   Star wouldn't calm herself to hear anything that Darren had to say. Star wasn't giving Darren no room or no chance to explain himself. Actually at that very moment, Star didn't want to hear nothing that Darren had to say.   Star was in the process of overthinking.   It was so many things going through her head as fast a freight train. Star couldn't keep it straight. One minute she was tripping over this and the next moment she was tripping over that. Whatever was on her mind at that very time, Star had no problem letting it come out of her mouth with no filter.

Star seemed as if she was having hot flashes as well as mood swings.She was starting to sweat as she continued to yell at Darren as he got dressed, Star had noticed that Darren was putting on his clothes but that didn't stop her from saying what she wanted to say. It also didn't alter the way that Star was feeling. It actually mad Star feel worst because during this tirade, Darren was getting dressed to leave. Star didn't know what to do, let alone what to say. She didn't want to seem vulnerable or weak so she stood her ground, thinking as well as believing that she was showing her strength.

Without speaking any more words, Darren headed toward the door. As soon as Star turned her back and began yelling at the top of her lungs again, Darren crept right out of the door without Star even noticing. By the time Star noticed that Darren wasn't in the room anymore, she searched their house only to come to the conclusion that Darren had left and was gone. Leaving Star all alone with her problems only to be yelling at herself. Leaving Star all alone by herself with only her thoughts.

Now that Star was alone, she quit yelling and began to cry. While Darren was there with her she held her composure and kept it together but now that Darren was gone, Star just let everything out. The pain. The lies. The deceit.

The miscommunication.   The frustration.   The disbelief.   Star was now trapped in her own grief without Darren there to help her. Star was really feeling some type of way.   Darren had walked out and left Star without any words or reactions.   He was just gone.   Star knew that Darren leaving was something of her own making but the cause of the problem that Star was having was caused by Darren. Star had begun her spiral downward into depression.

   One of the ways Star had gotten over a lot of things was by being verbal.   Releasing her pain, thoughts and or whatever that she was going through with words. It also helped that Darren would be there to listen as well as help Star by giving her positive advice but now he was gone. Star didn't know what to do so she walked into their bedroom and fell onto their bed to sob into the pillows. Star didn't know why Darren had left but she did understand that Darren had left because of the commotion that was going on but everything that was going on was a straight effect of what Darren had caused.

"How could he walk out on me like I had did something wrong? Why was Darren acting as if it wasn't his problem as well as something that he had caused or participated in? What was really going on? Did Darren really care about Star? Or care to explain to Star what was really going on?" So many thoughts were running through Star's head. She laid in their king size crying her whole heart out. Star had come this far only by Faith and believing in the Almighty GOD HIMSELF. Also by the support that Darren would physically as well as emotionally give her.

Chapter Three

What was she going to do now? This was one of the greatest moments in her life that Star felt that she needed someone to be there for her and now she had no one. No one to cry to or cry on. No one to catch or wipe her tears away. No one to console her and tell her that everything was going to be okay. No one to tell or show her that she was worth the risk and consequences. There was no one. Star was all alone once again in her life. This made Star feel some type of way. Star was emotionally frustrated and didn't know how to handle it or herself. Star didn't know what to do. Al she knew was that she wanted this feeling to leave and be gone. Never to return again any more in her life.

Star was breaking down and she could tell. She felt any hope of being as happy as she was before slipping right through her fingers. Nomatter how tight she held her hands closed. She had worked so hard to get to the point of being happy and content with herself as well as the things and people in her life and now it was all gone. She felt that she was somehow deceived by the man that she was supposed to be in love with and was soon to be married to.

The more Star thought about it, the harder she cried. Star felt weak. Weak because she felt that she fell into the trap that Darren had set for her. He had to have known what was going on. How did he know of Star? How did he end up in Star's life? There were so many things running through her mind.

Star was back to overthinking again because Darren wasn't there to give her any answers to any of the questions that she had. She had to just assume what was going on and everything going through her head was negative. Star instantly started feeling depressed. After all that she had went through in her life. She thought all that was over when she met Darren. Not knowing or thinking that he would add to the bad moments or memories in her life. Star fell out in the middle of the room. Weak in the knees was just a phrase until Star actually experienced it for herself and that was just part of what she was going through. All of the crying had made Star feel as if she was weak.

Weak physically because she had no strength to move nor did she want to.   At that moment, Star just wanted to crawl up into a ball and die. Star felt weak emotionally because after all she had experienced in her life, this was just adding to it. Star felt weak emotionally because she felt that she had done everything right and in her power to never ever have this feeling and feel this way again but here she was going through it.

Star summoned up the strength to get back up to her feet and headed straight for the living room.   Once in the living room, Star walked over to the cabinet where Darren kept all the liquor in the house.   The liquor was for the company when they came over to watch the game and when he would have any type of gambling party when he was home.

Tonight didn't include any company, any game and or any gambling.   It just included Star and her sorrows.   Star wasn't a heavy drinker and barely drunk hard liquor.   She was more of a wine person but tonight Star felt as if it was well deserved and that she wanted it.   She wantedand needed to get lost in the whole bottle of the first liquor she grabbed which was a fifth of Redberry Ciroc. She just wanted to escape reality and hopefully this liquor would help her to feel better. Star was the first to open the bottle because everything had been restocked for the upcoming Superbowl party that they were supposed to have. Once Star opened the bottle, she didn't hesitate and went all the way in. Hitting the bottle from the neck.

Star could feel the liquor as it traveled through her body. From her mouth down her throat to her stomach. Star was experiencing a burning sensation but that didn't stop Star from taking another swig. After a few more shots, Star could feel the effects that the liquor was having on her body.It was making her feel woozy as well as light-headed. It kind of sort of made Star feel a little better. Atleast a little bit anyway but it was somehow helping in her moment of pain. Before Star knew it, she was back in her room, laid on top of the bed sobbing uncontrollably again. Star was falling apart and she knew it. She just couldn't pull herself together.

Before Star knew it, she had fallen asleep crying and had to have been in a deep sleep because she had slept all night. When she woke up it was almost afternoon. Star rolled over to check her phone. When she looked at it, there were no missed calls. Meaning that Darren hadn't even tried to get in touch with her. No phone call. No voicemail. Not even a text message was sent. Out of the whole time that Star had known Darren, this was their first disagreement. This was their first argument. Their first fight. This was the first time that they had experienced anything but happiness together. All of Star's happy moments in life was provided and produced by Darren.

Darren had done everything right up until the moment when he walked out on Star. He was the only person there for Star whenever she had any bad days in life and now he was nowhere to be found. Where was Darren and what was going on with him? How was he feeling because Star was feeling like shit. With no answers to the questions that Star had and with Darren nowhere in site, Star was left to assume what was going on as well as what was going to happen. Star felt deceived by Darren. Obviously Darren knew something about what had happened to Star when she was younger or he wouldn't have reacted the way that he did.

Darren had to have known something or he wouldn't have left. Something was really going on and Star felt that she was right in the middle of a conspiracy. Something that had happened and somebody wanted to keep it swept under a rug for nobody to find out. Star had so many things going through her head. She knew at that moment that she was in her stage of overthinking but she couldn't help herself. She had a lot of unanswered questions. Star could feel her blood starting to boil the more. She felt her temperature rise as she became frustrated once again.

Star jumped to her feet, rushed over to her walk in closet and began grabbing her clothes and garments. Throwing all items on the bed. Then she walked into the kitchen's pantry and grabbed the unfolded boxes that they had stored from the time they had moved into the house and made her way back to their room where she proceeded to throw her clothing into the boxes sitting at the closets door.

All this was done in a moment of haste and frustration because once Star came to realization of the reality that they were in, that she was in, she realized that she had nowhere to go as well as no one to go to. Star had no family as well as no friends so there was no place for her to run to for a couple days and no one to help her out in her time of need.

That was another thing that mad Star upset. Knowing that she had no one else to depend on was very frustrating now that her and Darren was going through this situation.   In their moments of happiness and pure bliss there was no need to have such a thing because their communication with one another was impeccable. They talked and discussed almost everything.   The good things, the bad things.   Sometimes even the things in-between.   That is another reason Star was threw off and more confused when Darren walked out on her.   It made her think more as to what was the reason that Darren couldn't answer the questions that she had.

That was the reason that Star automatically assumed that Darren knew way more than he had told Star previously or played a part in what had happened to her in life. There was something deeper. Something bigger than her. Something that was so important that it couldn't be spoken about or that they, he, Darren didn't want anybody to know. Star began to think about her mother and what had happened to her.

Could that have been the reason that her mother was killed? Could that have been the reason why no one was ever brought to justice for the murder of her mother. Because it was being covered up? Star was starting to become paranoid. Would Darren try to have Star killed? Because she had now uncovered a secret that he did not want Star to know. Or would he try to kill Star himself?

Star instantly became scared for her life. It was one thing to be angry because she felt as if she was being lied to. But it was something totally different to think that those lies could affect her life or put her in a life and death situation. Star grabbed her True Religion duffle bag from the top shelf in her closet and threw a couple items into the bag. All the things that she felt she would need because she was going to stay at a hotel or something. Star thought that now that her life was in jeopardy, so she wasn't staying another night in the place where Darren knew to find her. She just had to leave. So she did.

Upon arriving at the hotel, Star hadn't talked or spoken to anyone since Darren had walked out on her, so the refreshing spirit that the lady at the counter had was way more than needed as well as invited. It was more than wanted and it added a ray of sunshine to Star's already gloomy world. Star walked up to the desk where the young lady was standing and swallowed all that was bothering her as she began to talk. The whole encounter didn't last no more than ten minutes. As she booked a hotel stay for a couple nights, not knowing exactly how long this would be going on.

Star stopped every now and again to check to make sure that no one was following her in the direction that she was going. Once she made it to her room number, she looked both ways before she slid the key card through the kiosk. This stage of paranoid thoughts was really starting to get to Star. She had left the house to only end up at a room just to make sure Darren didn't know where she was. Just in case he was trying or going to send someone to harm her. But it didn't change what had happen or the things that she was going through. Mentally or emotionally.

The room was in no comparison to the condo that they stayed in. In fact the hotel room was about as big as their living room but Star wasn't in the shape or form to be in the mood for complaining. Star was happy to just feel safe at that moment. She threw her bag on the bed and began to unpack the things that she had brought with her. Once she was done, she went into the bathroom to run herself a hot bubble bath so that she could calm her nerves and relax. When the bath was finish, Star took off her clothes and got in. As every part of her body entered the steamy hot water, Star could feel her muscles loosening up. She could feel the tenseness of her body falling away as she placed her head on the headrest at the back of the tub.

Chapter Four

Star sat in the tub until the water became cool then let some of it out while running more hot water. Star didn't want to get out. She just wanted to stay there for the rest of the day or atleast until she got her mind right on what she was to do next. As Star tried to relax again, all the things that she called herself trying to forget or distance herself from came rushing back to her as if it was a tsunami wave rushing back through her mind. Star began to feel as if she was overwhelmed again. She started crying harder than she had cried previously. To the point that she felt as if she couldn't catch her breathe.

Star felt as if she was having a nervous breakdown. Everything was going haywire right at the moment that everything was supposed to be perfect. All the good times and days that the two of them had shared with one another was now just a memory at the moment. Star thought to herself that she didn't want to have nothing to do with Darren now that she was feeling the way that he had made her feel. But how could he?   Star still had questions for Darren whether they got back together or not.   Star had questions that she wanted and needed to ask and she also wanted the answers to them from the one and only person she felt could give them.

Straight from the horse's mouth and the only one that could give them to her was Darren.   The time and the place that all of this was to take place was up in the air. Star hadn't called Darren and vice versa.   There was no verbal communication going on between the two of them. No phone calls, no voicemails, not even a text message. Star was beginning to take this fallout personal because it seemed as if Darren was taking this out on her by not having any contact with her. Like she herself had done something to him or done something wrong. But why would Darren feel this way. The two of them had never really had any type of arguments or had never even fallen out with one another.

Their relationship was nothing but pure bliss up until the moment that Darren had stepped out the shower and crossed the threshold of the bedroom door to find Star there waiting with an angry look upon her face.   Everyday that they had spent together was filled with happiness as well as making each other happy and comfortable. Darren had heard the stories of Star's past and the things that she had went through.   Darren had promised to not hurt Star and to always keep a smile upon her face. Star knew deep down that Darren had nothing but her best interest at heart and she felt that Darren wouldn't do anything to hurt her purposely.

This is why the whole time that they were together was nothing but a dream come true. As well as the main reason why Star wanted to take Darren's last name.   Another one of the reasonsthat the two were to be married, but with all of this drama going on, Star couldn't really focus on the wedding.   Especially now that they were not speaking to one another.

Star didn't know where their situation or relationship was headed.   Star didn't even know what she was going to do about the situation that she was now in.

Star just knew that she wanted answers. The answers to all the questions that she had. Nomatter if it would hurt her or not. Star wanted to know. Star felt that she had to know.

It would be the only way for Star to get over the pain and be able to move forward. Star thought all her bad days were behind her. She would have never thought or imagined that this would happen to her. The worst part of the whole incident was being hurt or deceived by the one person that she thought she could trust. Deceived by the only person that she felt she could count on. Deceived by the person she was in love with, the one person that she was to marry and spend the rest of her life with. The one person that she thought wouldn't do anything to hurt her or make her feel like this.

The first couple of days, Star didn't leave the room or even make any phone calls. Star just wanted to be alone. She needed and wanted time to herself to atleast try to help herself in understanding the situation to the best of her ability. She needed this time to get her mind right and get back to herself because to her, Star felt that she was tripping. Assuming as well as over reacting but at the same time, everything also seemed justified.   Star didn't know what was going on anymore and now that she was back to being alone she had no one there to confirm that this was just one rainy day and that everything would be alright.   That is what Darren always did for her.

Star was all discombobulated. Her mind was everywhere but where it was supposed to be.   Star couldn't stay focused, it was so much going on her head.   So much running through her mind.   This situation was actually eating Star alive.   Star could feel herself falling back into her stages of depression. She even felt suicidal at times. Feeling like she just wanted to end it all.   Star felt as if her life was filled with tragedy, misery and that it wasn't worth living.   Especially if she was going to keep going through the things that didn't make her happy.   Or brought her to the point of where she was at that very moment in time.

Star just felt that she wanted to let go.   Releasing all the things that made her feel the way that she was feeling. As well as the people and things that continued to haunt and hurt her. Leaving it all behind. No more crying. No more stress. No more cares. No more worries. As Star came to this conclusion, she thought of the many ways to commit suicide. She knew that she could hang herself, shoot herself in the head, slit her wrist or over overdose with prescription medication. Star wanted to kill herself but she wanted to do so in the least painful way possible.

So she started her bath water as she scrambled through her bag looking for the medication she had packed up when she left the condo. She looked at the bottle of pills that she was getting ready to consume and read it over as if it was prescribed to her. The bottle of prescribed drugs said to take a total of no more than four pills in a twenty-four hour period and to not mix this drug with alcohol. Star opened the bottle and poured the contents of the bottle into the palm of her hand.

There was a good count of atleast thirty pills. Star walked over to the mini fridge that was in her the room and open the door to grab the bottle of liquor from the top shelf and opened it. In one hand was the alcoholic beverage and in the other hand was a fistful of medication. Star walked back into the bathroom where she had already made her bath water. With just a t-shirt on, Star entered the tub filled with water. While sitting up, Star looked from hand to hand to take one last glimpse of what she was about to do to herself but continued anyway.

Without another thought, Star popped the pills into her mouth and washed them down with the whole bottle of alcohol that was in her other hand. Star could feel her that her body wasn't as tense as it had previously been and that her mind was at a state of almost relaxation. Star could feel that she was slipping away and as she did, she closed her eyes and released her cares into the universe.

As Star slipped away into the darkness of her mind, she lost all consciousness of the reality of the world. All senses were gone. No feeling. No smell. No taste. So forth and so on. When Star was able to gain control of her body again, she realized that her attempt to kill herself had failed and that now she was laid in a bed in the hospital. Star was right back where she started. Opening her eyes was easy but her vision was blurry and she could barely move her body, let alone feel it. Star couldn't even speak because of the tube that the doctors had placed down her throat to help her breathe.

Star didn't know where she was at first because of her blurry eye sight. She couldn't see anything, feel anything, let alone hear anything so Star thought that she had made it to the other side successfully until she felt something lodged in her throat which made her start to choke. Upon gagging and the heavy breathing that she was experiencing, it made her heart rate go up which ultimately set off the machine to alert the nurses in the other room, whom quickly rushed into the room to aid the choking patient. When the nurses noticed that Star was woke, one rushed off to get a fellow doctor that was on duty to assist.

By the time the doctor arrived in the room, the other nurse had already begun to sedate Star so that she would calm down by injecting a drug into her IV. Star was now relaxed enough for the tube to be taken out of her throat. The tube was only placed there to help her breath because when Star was brought into the hospital, she could not breathe on her own.Star was in a drug induced coma because of the incident of her trying to kill herself. The doctors had to pump her stomach to rid Star's body of all medicine and toxins that she had consumed. Waking up in the hospital again brought back all the bad memories that Star was trying to forget.

Seemed that Star was right back where she had started this journey called life by trying to end hers. All the things that Star was trying to escape in reality, seemed to keep finding their way back into the scene. All the things that Star wanted to leave in her past kept reintroducing themselves into her presence. Star just wanted to forget all the bad things that had happened. All the things that made her feel some type of way. That was one of the reasons that she had contemplated suicide and went about killing herself.

The doctor walked over to the bed where Star was laid and began to look over her. He checked her eyes to see if she had any activity of the pupil, which means she was alert and coherent. Then he checked her breathing by placing the stethoscope first on her back then moving it around toward the front, ending at her chest. Star's breathing had become stable without the breathing tube so the next thing was to check the response of her reflexes. Once the doctor was finish with all the tests and things that he wanted done for Star, than he pulled up a chair right along the bedside and begin to address Star.

The doctor explained to Star why she was brought into the hospital for. The doctor explained to Star all the procedures that they had done on and to her to save her life. Including the pumping of her stomach and drug induced coma. The conversation was only one sided because Star had yet to utter any word out of her mouth. At that moment, the doctor was doing all the talking.

The doctor explained to Star how close she was to death before she made it to the hospital and how blessed she was to be alive. The doctor told Star that she had been in the hospital for three to four weeks. He also explained to Star that they had taken blood from her to be tested and that is when they discovered that Star was with child. Actually almost two months pregnant. Seven and a half weeks to be exact.

Star looked up at the doctor whom was seated to her left and gave him the look of surprise as if to say, "Huh?" The doctor stood to his feet, grabbed Star by her hand and shook it as if to say congratulations, then walked out of the room on his way to assist the other patients. Star fell back onto the pillow used to help sit her up and replayed the words that had just come out of the doctor's mouth.

Overand over again Star could hear what the doctor had said to her so clear as if he was still sitting on her bedside. After the moments of excitement left the room, the feelings of doubt crept back in. Star started to doubt what the doctor had told her because she had learned when she was at the age of sixteen that she wasn't able to conceive a child. Let alone be and get pregnant.

Star begin to think that maybe the doctor had mixed her results up with someone else's and maybe he had read the wrong name or atleast the wrong results. It was sure to be a miracle for sure if Star was pregnant especially after all the things she had went throughin her teenage years . After all this time, thinking that she couldn't and wouldn't be able to conceive, Star had given up the idea of being a mother. Let alone had she even tried to see if she could get pregnant. Star had just journeyed over the threshold of being in her thirties and never in her life had she been pregnant at all. Star had a glimmer of hope shining ever so brightly inside her and didn't even know it.

But she didn't want to geek herself up for failure or start to believe that she was pregnant when she really wasn't. After a few days of being able to breathe on her own, Star was then up and walking as well as formulating the words to make a sentence. The doctors were all amazed at the progress that Star had made in her recovery over the last few days.

Some thought that it was remarkable. Star had let the thoughts of motherhood stand close to the back of the line of questions that she had and wanted answered before they discharged her. Once everything was taken care of, Star couldn't help but ask the question about her pregnancy.

Chapter Five

The nurse reassured her that it was true and just to prove to Star that they were not telling a lie, they ordered another pregnancy test to be conducted on Star's urine as well as her blood. When the nurse came in, she walked in smiling reading that the results from both test were the same indicating that Star was indeed pregnant. Star wanted to believe what the nurses as well as what the doctor had told her was true but she couldn't. Star felt that this could be another cruel joke that was being played in her life. It was one thing to say something but it was another thing to actually see it, so the nurse arraigned for Star to have an ultrasound before she left the facility.

The day that Star was due to be discharged, the nurse came by her room to pick her up and escort her to the room where the ultrasound would take place. After dropping Star off in the room and telling her to get undressed from the waist down. The nurse closed the door only to reenter it with the machine and the technician who would run it. Star was nervous to say the least because she didn't know what was going on or what was about to happen. This was Star's first time experiencing what was going on. The positive results. The pregnancy. The ultrasound. All of these things were new to Star.

As Star laid upon the examination table, with her pants unfastened and down to her waist and with her shirt pulled up to cover her chest but expose her stomach, Star thought to herself about the possibility of being with child and how it would make her so happy to have life growing inside of her. Star wanted for the results to be true for more reasons than that. One reason being that the new life would give her the reason to keep her own life. To care more for her own self and to take care of herself. With new life comes many responsibility.

The technician turned the ultrasound machine on and waited for it to boot itself up. While waiting on the machine, the technician prepped Star by covering Star's chest with a white towel as well as her bottom half. The technician grabbed a tube of clear liquid and squirted it on Star's belly. Below her belly button then took the scope and began to move it around her stomach. Starting where the clear solution was. As the technician moved the scope around, he looked at the monitor on the machine and every now and again he pressed a button to snap a screen shot of the image he was looking at.

After a few screen shots, the technician turned the monitor around so that Star could see what, if anything, that the technician was observing and looking at. When the tech turned the screen toward Star, she couldn't see anything but the black and white screen that resembled when you would turn on the television and the antenna wasn't connected to it but once the tech placed the scope back upon Star's stomach there was a blotch of something that appeared upon the screen. The technician began explaining to Star what was going on as well as what it was that the two of them were looking at.

The technician spoke to Star saying, "This here is your fetus. It is still a fetus because you are only in the first trimester. Embarking upon eight weeks. So you as well as the fetus are new to this journey and you will need to take better care of yourself if you want to bring a healthy child into this world." Star looked at the screen with astonishment and amazement.

Surprised, thrilled and anxious all at the same time. She couldn't believe what she was hearing, let alone what it was that she was seeing but she believed that it had to have been the truth. It was now believable to Star. She had heard about it but now she had the chance to see it. Witness the new life, the beginning stages of life with her own two eyes.

Star was literally overjoyed with the news that she was

pregnant and now had the opportunity to bring a child into the world. Excited that she had the chance to be a mother and the opportunity to experience motherhood. This is one of the moments that all women waited for and wanted in their lifetime of being on earth. The other was to experience a relationship of love and be married. Star was thrilled with the thought of being a parent and having someone else to share her love and her life with. After the technician was finish with the ultrasound, he wished Star the best on her new addition and exited the room so that Star could put her clothes back on.

As Star lay upon the table, she began to imagine things about the baby she was carrying. She thought about how the baby would look. What was she going to name the baby? As well as what the sex of the baby was going to be. All that really was of a concern to Star was being able to carry the baby to full term and delivery a healthy child. This was truly a miracle Star thought to herself as she recognized the blessing that GOD had placed in her life, right when she needed it.

A breakthrough was far from overdue.

Star stood to her feet as she fastened her clothes. Once she was dressed, Star stood in the middle of the floor, placed both her hands across her stomach and stared up at the ceiling. With her eyes closed, Star prayed to GOD. Thanking HIM for the blessing that HE had bestowed upon her as well as her life. This was truly a new beginning for Star. A time to change all the negatives into positives. Her downs into ups. Her frown into a smile. Her lefts into rights. A new beginning at the chance of living life more abundantly.

When Star exited the room where they had given her the ultrasound, she entered the hallway and walked down the hallway until she saw the sign saying exit. There was a room filled with people before Star came upon the exit so Star stopped to look in and be nosey about what was going on in there. On the door of the room was Star's name on a tag that said please enter. When Star entered the room she noticed that she didn't know any of the people that were standing around and she only recognized maybe atleast two of them from her time of being at the hospital.

Then Star saw the nurse whom had been at her bedside since the moment she opened her eyes and noticed where it is she was. The nurse walked over to Star holding a miniature cake that read, "Congratulations," on it. At that very moment everyone looked toward Star and yelled, "Surprise!" Star instantly burst out into tears. Crying tears of happiness and joy. This was so beautiful and well needed for Star and she knew it. She could feel the electricity in the atmosphere and it made Star feel more love for herself as well as her unborn child.

Star felt overwhelmed with the compassion that everyone was showering her with. Especially knowing how she had ended up in the hospital in the first place. Star now knew that her life had more meaning than she could have ever imagined. All these people who barely knew Star was showering she with love and that also made Star feel some type of way. Each person in the room took the time to personally touch, shake her hand or hug Star as well as to congratulate her on her upcoming arrival. When everyone were finished embracing Star, the nurse that had taken care of Star while she was in the hospital stood in front of the crowd of people to thank them for their participation in making this a successful event.

They didn't have time or knew Star personally enough to rush out and get gifts so they just gave Star what they could, which was the love that she had received as well as a couple of gift cards so that Star could have some type of help in preparing for the arrival of her unborn child. Star collected all the items that she was given and thanked everyone that stood in the room as well. Especially the nurse.

With tears in her eyes and rolling down her cheeks, Star looked toward the nurse and explained why this meant so much to her. By the end of her speech, basically the whole room was in tears. The nurse joined Star in front of the room and embraced Star one more time as she whispered in Star's ear, "Now that is your testimony! You must go to the highest mountain and shout it to the world. Tell somebody! Anybody! Everybody!"

The nurse kissed Star on her cheek, grabbed her by her hand and thanked everyone once more before everyone departed the room to get back to work. The nurse and Star continued to talk as the nurse walked Star toward the exit. Before the two departed from each other, the nurse gave Star her phone number and told her to call if she needed anything.

Then the nurse rephrased what she said and told Star to call if she needed anyone to talk to or just anything period. At the moment, the alarm of the hospital started going off. Alerting the nurses that the EMS had arrived with a patient in a trauma situation. Good thing was that Star's nurse was already at the door when the Paramedics arrived, rushing the patient in.

Star stood toward the side of the room to make sure that she didn't get run over when the Paramedics came rushing through the door. The nurse jumped right in to assist the Paramedics with the patient. Star stood off to the side of the door as they flew right past her. Glancing only to get a glimpse of the person on the gurney. Star couldn't believe her eyes. As they rushed the patient into the operating room, Star could have sworn that this person looked like Darren. Matter of fact, Star was quite sure of it. Star was sure that it was indeed Darren so she decided to stay at the hospital to find out any information on what had happened to him as well as was he going to be okay.

Star sat still in one spot as she waited for her favorite nurse to come out so that she would be able to ask her questions about the situation with Darren. As Star sat there, the waiting room filled up with all types of people. From people trying to register to be seen by the emergency doctors to the people who were coming to check on their family, friends and loved ones. There was an elderly couple that resembled Darren that walked in, didn't ask any questions or say who they were there to see and sat off a few rows behind Star. But Star wasn't quite sure if these two were his parents or not. Knowing that they had never met before or been formerly introduced.

When Star's favorite nurse came out of the operating room, her smocks were all messed up. Covered with blood from the patient she was just assisting the doctors with. That Star thought it to be Darren. Star rushed over to the nurse to ask questions about what was going on with the patient that the nurse had just left. The nurse was a little bit standoffish to give Star any information. Being that the nurse didn't know what was going on. The nurse informed Star that she couldn't release any information at that time because she had none to give plus the nurse could only notify the immediate family about what was going on with the patient.

Star tried to explain to the nurse that she knew the patient and that the patient was actually the father of her unborn child. The nurse looked at Star with a look as if she was surprised at what she had just heard Star say. But either way it went or was going, the nurse still told Star that she couldn't tell her anything about or on the patient because she was not the patient's immediate family. Star started to go ballistic. Raising her voice and all as she explained once again that the patient is the father of her unborn child and that she just wanted to know if he was alright or going to be alright.

The nurse explained again to Star that she could not give out any information to anyone that was not the patient's immediate family as far as mother, father, brother, sister or wife. The nurse also explained to Star that even if she was carrying the patient's unborn child that did not entitle her to receive or be told what was going on with him. That at that moment Star was just a babymother and kept walking.

Star looked at the nurse as she walked away in disbelief.

Chapter Six

Star became upset but as she stomped back to her seat, she realized that her being upset was no good for the baby so she tried to calm herself down as she began to think peaceful thoughts about the arrival of their unborn child. The more Star tried to calm herself down, the more she upset herself because she didn't know what was going on with Darren. Star didn't know if Darren was going to make it or if the situation was serious to where he wouldn't make it. All this made Star emotional because as she thought to herself she also thought about Darren dying before he could find out that he had a child on the way.

This situation also reminded Star of where this all started and how immature it was of the two of them to not be able to talk about or talk through their problems. It had been a minute since Darren had stormed out of their condo never to be seen or heard from again until Star saw him on that gurney. The thoughts made Star feel sick to her stomach so she got up and rushed to the bathroom because she felt as if she had to vomit.   When Star was coming out of the restrooms, she saw the nurse coming around the bend so she got herself together to inquire about the patient again.

The nurse stopped to listen to Star but once again explained to her what the hospital policy was and that if she broke the policy that it was a chance that she could get reported or worse, even fired. The nurse also explained to Star that the policy was strict and was to be adhered to.   One of the main reasons was because the hospital had cameras in every room, shooting from every angle.   Star felt that maybe if the nurse knew the whole story that maybe, just maybe she would be inclined to help Star with just a little bit of information.

Star pulled the nurse to the side of the room and began to explain why she was determined to learn what was going on with that patient. Star started from her childhood and growing up without any parents. That her mother was murdered when Star was a very young child. Star explained all the things that had happened to her in her teenage years to where she was told that she would never be able to conceive a child even in her later years but somehow now being pregnant was some kind of miracle. Star continued by telling the nurse how she had met Darren and how he had helped her through her darkest moments in life and that is how she fell in love with him.

Star also explained to the nurse about the last time the two of them had seen each other they had a big fallen out to where they hadn't seen or even spoken to each other since. That seeing Darren arriving to the hospital was her first time seeing him in almost two months. The nurse looked at Star with a little bit of sympathy in her eyes as she listened to what Star was telling her. Once Star was finished telling the nurse her whole life story, you could see it in the nurse's eyes that she wanted to help Star. Especially after hearing everything that Star had went through to make it to this moment in her life.

The nurse told Star that the only way that she could help her at that moment in time was to mention her name to the patient. If or when he woke up from surgery. To see if they did indeed know of each other and to see his response. At that moment the emergency alarms starting going off again and a female voice came over the P.A. system to announce that all nurses on hand and in the building needed to report to the operating room to assist. Star felt her heart drop as she saw the nurses rushing through the O.R. door. Star didn't know what was going on and as she stood there she started to assume the worst so Star bowed her head as the tears swelled up in her eyes, then she looked up toward the ceiling to begin praying to GOD.

Star didn't want this to be the end of her and Darren. Not before she had the chance to see or talk again with him in good spirits. Star didn't want this to be the end for Darren now that she had found out that she was pregnant with his child. Star wanted to be the one to tell Darren the great news of their upcoming arrival. She was sure that it would shock as well as surprise him at the same time. Star was willing to put what they were going through to the side for sake of the positivity that was needed at that moment. So she decided to pray.

Star started her prayer off by asking for forgiveness. Forgiveness for herself first, because she knew that the only time she prayed or talked to GOD was to always ask something of HIM. Star explained to GOD that she would come to HIM more often if HE would grant her this one wish. Which was to make sure that everything went well with Darren's surgery and that he would be okay.

Star also explained to GOD that if HE chose to grant Star this very wish that she would use every opportunity to acknowledge, praise, uplift as well as tell everyone she came into contact with about her testimony and what GOD had done for her. Whether her days were good or bad. Whether she had the time or not.

As Star closed out her prayer, she could feel the pressure being lifted from her as well as hear a voice telling her, "GOD has this under control. Trust in HIM." The voice actually sounded like Star's mother and it left Star feeling a little bit more comforted. Star had finally realized at that moment that she really, really loved this man and that she wasn't ready to let him go. Despite what was going on and what had happened. Star was still madly in love with Darren and she was willing to do whatever it took to keep it that way as well as him in her life. Even if that meant that she had to forgive him for whatever it is or was that he had done to her to keep her from finding out the truth.

Star was ready to forgive Darren and move forward with their life now that all of this had happened. Plus Darren had given Star the greatest thing in the world. With Darren, Star had experienced the greatness that the world had to offer. Which was love, happiness and now a child of her very own. Star felt better now that she had talked with and had a conversation with GOD. HE assured Star that she had not nothing to be worried about now that she had placed everything in GOD's hand.

Star had been discharged from the hospital and was free to go home but decided that she wasn't leaving the hospital until she knew that everything was okay with Darren so she went back to the waiting room and made herself at home. Waiting for any word from the nurse about Darren's condition and or his response to the nurse telling him that Star was outside in the waiting room.

Before Star knew it, three days had passed before there was any word from the nurse. All the while waiting, Star stayed at the hospital. Day & night. Waiting. Finally the nurse came & woke Star up from what she would have said to have been a dream but now that Star was awake, she knew it wasn't a dream. It was actually a reality what Star was going through. The pregnancy as well as the situation with Darren being in the hospital.

Sometimes to Star it actually felt as if she was going out of mind. Insane. Everytime Star felt as if she was three or so steps ahead of herself in life, she was thrown a curve ball that knocked atleast seven steps back and landed her right back where she was trying not to go. To the space that she knew wasn't any good for her and now it was no good for her nor her unborn child.

Star just felt the need to be there for Darren regardless of what they were going through and whatever they had went through. The blessings of a new life. The blessings of a child was more than enough for Star and Darren to realize that they had bigger and more important things to worry about and put their energy into.

The nurse was helpful the whole time Star was at the hospital. Bringing Star a blanket and a pillow to sleep with. Making sure that she had something to eat as well as making sure Star took her prenatal pills for the baby. When the nurse nudged Star to wake her up, she had a smile on her face. Star looked up at her and asked her what time it was. The nurse simply replied that it was time for her to be able to see Darren.

Star instantly stood to her feet and fixed her clothes as well as her hair. As Star swiped her hair behind her ear, she asked the nurse, "How do I look?" The nurse looked back at Star and replied, "Beautiful! As you should. Now come on so I can get you back here." The nurse ushered Star through two automatic doors that people needed a badge to get pass.

After walking down a few hallways and a couple of lefts and rights, they came to a door of a room. The nurse looked to Star and said to her, "This is where I leave you two alone." Kissed Star on the cheek and told her, "I will be here if ever you need anything. Remember that. Always!" Then the nurse turned and walked away. Leaving Star staring and standing at the door.

Star gathered herself as well as her thoughts before she entered the room. Finally she would be able to see Darren. Be around him, spend time with him as well as talk to him. Star finally would have the time to tell Darren that she was pregnant and that the two of them were expecting.

Star entered the room and tried not to make any noise because it looked as if Darren was sleeping and Star didn't want to wake him up. Just the sight of Darren made Star's heart flutter as if this was the first time they had met and were seeing each other. The sight of Darren had given Star butterflies in the pit of stomach. At that moment of Star looking into Darren's face is when she finally realized how much that she missed and love that man.

As Star stood over the bedside of Darren, she rubbed her hand over his head, than leaned in to kiss him on the forehead. When Star stood back up she realized that Darren was awake and staring back at her. "Hey stranger!" Darren said to Star. Instantly a smile flashed across Star's face. She was happy that Darren had woke up and she was also happy that he was now back to speaking to her.

The last time the two of them had seen each other, they were not on good terms. With Darren waking up in good spirits, it was a good sign that they were on the right track to atleast being cordial with each other. Plus Star had some good news that she wanted to share with Darren and that made the situation even better for the upcoming announcement that she was going to make.

As the two of them conversed with one another, they talked about all the things that had been going on since the last time they had seen one another. Darren mostly talked about business because that was all that he ever did and was consumed with. Star talked mostly about her mental and emotional state since the last time they had seen each other.

Then Darren took it amongst himself to ask Star, "Do you miss me?" Without waiting for Star to answer, he said to her, "Because I missed you!" With a smile across his face. Darren began to explain to Star how everything had seemed to be going wrong since the two of them had fallen out. He also was trying to answer some of the questions that Star had asked him before he walked out on her.

Explaining to Star that a lot that happened in the past he had inherited through his family when he decided to join the family business. A lot of the things that had happened in the past were to be kept secret and not told to anyone including Darren himself. Once he had taken the time to understand what was going on and what Star was yelling about during their argument, it opened his eyes to many things that had been going on in the business. His family business.

At the moment of the commotion he had no time to

think so he just reacted by leaving to let the situation calm down. But as Darren began to think about what Star was saying to him, he took it upon himself to start checking records and looking into the backlogs of the family company and that also started commotion in his family. Which is one of the reasons that he ended up where he was at that moment which was in the hospital.

Star looked at Darren as he continued to talk to her. In the midst of one of his statements Star blurted out, "So your family tried to kill you too?" Star looked at

Darren with the deer caught in the headlights face and waited for his response.   Darren quickly answered, "No, of course not. Why would they do that?   Why would they want to hurt me? Why would they want to hurt their own son?"

Star looked Darren straight in the face and replied, "For the same reason that they could have had my mother murdered."   Darren looked back at Star and said, " What?   You have no proof of that. And besides when I was shot, my parents were out of town on vacation.   Star continued looking at Darren as he spoke and once he was finished talking and or had taken a breath to begin his next sentence she said to him, "Out of town?" With a strange look on her face. "How were your parents out of town on vacation when you got shot but they were in the waiting room soon after they rushed you in?"

To Star something wasn't adding up but she wasn't sure if it was the situation not adding up or if it wasn't adding up because that is what Darren wanted her to believe. Either way it was, Star was still happy that Darren was going to be alright and pull through.   Darren continued to talk about the incident that lead up to the him being shot.   He said, "A lot of the things that were to be kept in the past, my parents never told me anything about.   Not one single detail did I know until I met you Star."

Star looked at Darren with a look of sympathy on her face. "Awwww!"   She thought to herself as she smiled on the inside. Darren continued, "I had been at the office all day doing some investigating on what you were saying and came across some files that were placed in an archive folder that was supposed to be deleted from my father's desktop. I scanned through the first few pages and thought to myself to print out the whole file before my dad returned to his office and found out what I was doing."

"After printing out the file, I left my dad's office and went back into my office to read what I had just printed out. Somewhere around the fourth or so page I saw your mother's name and instantly panicked. I couldn't believe what I was seeing. I couldn't believe what I was looking at. I couldn't believe that it may have been some truth to all the things you had been saying to me." Darren said.

"When I saw and recognized your mother's name, I began to pack up all my things for the day. I went back to the hotel and paced the floor for a few hours, wrecking my brain trying to figure out what had happened as well as what was now going on. That's when I received a phone call from my dad telling me that he and my mother were going out of town on a last minute, spare of the moment vacation just to get out of the city for a while.   Plus my mother wanted some quality time with my dad by herself because she could never pull him away from his work."

Chapter Seven

Star listened to Darren as he talked and the more he talked, the more it started to make sense to Star about what was going on and what had happened. It was also becoming very clear to Star that Darren could indeed be telling the truth to her now or maybe he had been telling the truth the whole time and really didn't know about anything that had happened to her mother as well as her in the past. Star was feeling really relieved in that moment of clarity.

But Star continued to listen to what Darren was saying. "After a day or so I was willing to put my pride and stubbornness to the side. I tried to contact you to talk about what was going on or atleast what I thought was going on but anytime I tried to call you, your phone went straight to the voicemail and I couldn't leave a message because your voicemail was full.

After a couple of more tries of trying to reach you, I decided to go by the condo to come and check up on you to make sure everything was alright. On my way to get into my car, somebody approached me from behind asking for my wallet and even after I gave it to him, he still shot me. Landing me here"

Star stared at Darren and in response to what he had just said to her, she replied, "I couldn't or didn't answer my phone because I was in the hospital for trying to kill myself." In the moment of Star speaking those words to Darren, something came over her and she begin to cry but continued talking. "I tried to kill myself by swallowing a whole bottle of prescription medication and drinking alcohol. I didn't know what else to do. I felt that everything that I had was lost or taken away from me so why not take my life."

Darren looked at Star as she cried, then grabbed Star by her hand and said to her, "Baby you will always have me!" Star took that moment and thought to herself, Wow!" At that moment Star let go a sigh of relief. Star said to Darren, "Babe, that's makes me feel so much better and alive inside. I love you!" Darren said, "I love you more Star." And the two of them passionately kissed each other as if sex was to follow. When Star went to wrap her arms around Darren as he lay in the bed, he let out a grunt as if in pain. "I'm sorry babe," Star said to Darren. "It's okay Star. I'm still sore from the surgery. I was shot three times in my torso and once in my back.

It was more like the man wanted me dead than he wanted my wallet and that's the fucked up part about this whole situation. Baby I could have been dead and never would have had the chance to see you, touch you, hold you, kiss you and tell you how much I love you. Star you have been my world ever since I first laid my eyes upon you and you mean the world to me and so much more. I don't want to fuss and fight with you ever again. I don't want to go another week, day, hour, minute or second without you. You win and will always win."

Star started to cry again but Darren told her, "Star you have nothing to worry about, I am here and I'm never going anywhere." As Darren wiped the falling tears from Star's face. Star looked at Darren and said, "I have something else I want to tell you," and with those words, Star gave Darren the pictures of the ultrasound. Darren looked very carefully at the what was just handed to him. With glee in his voice he exclaimed, "You mean to tell me that? You mean that you are? You mean that I am going to be a?" "Father. Yes babe!" Star replied to Darren as his eyes welled up with tears. Now both of them were crying but it was tears of joy of course.

As Star and Darren embraced one another, more people had entered Darren's room. The couple standing to the right of them were Darren's parents. When Darren and Star noticed that there were other people in the room, they fixed themselves to greet each other. As Darren introduced Star to his parents as his fiancé, their facial expression remained the same. There was not a glimmer of excitement in their face, in their eyes, let alone in their voice when they spoke.

Star stood there dumbfounded with her hand out to greet Darren's parents with a handshake but neither of them reciprocated the gesture. Star thought to herself of how rude they were being and acting. This was their first time seeing as well as meeting Star and they wouldn't and didn't atleast shake Star's hand. Darren's parents acted as if Star wasn't even in the room with them. Darren's mom ran to his bedside, cradling his face as she expressed how happy she was that Darren was alive. Darren's dad just stood there with a look of disgust on his face.

Darren's dad finally spoke aloud saying, "I would like to speak to my son alone for a moment. Excuse us please and exit the room." Then he looked in Star's direction, emphasizing that he was talking to her indirectly. Star grabbed Darren's hand and said to him as she begin to make her way toward the door, "I'm not going nowhere. I will be here if and when you need me."

As Star made her way toward the exit, she stared straight ahead. Making sure to not make eye contact with Darren's father. Darren's mother didn't look up or say anything. Once Star was on the other side of the door, she released a sigh and thought to herself that there was something strange going on with his family and she needed to find out what it exactly was. Star vowed to herself as well as her unborn child that she was going to get to the bottom of what was really going on.

Whether or not whomever wanted her to her or not.   Even if it killed them or not...........

www.ingramcontent.com/pod-product-compliance
Lightning Source LLC
Chambersburg PA
CBHW051243170626
46809CB00004B/1457